Studio Fun International
An imprint of Printers Row Publishing Group
A division of Readerlink Distribution Services, LLC
10350 Barnes Canyon Road, Suite 100, San Diego, CA 92121
www.studiofun.com

Printers Row Publishing Group is a division of Readerlink Distribution Services, LLC.
Studio Fun International is a registered trademark of Readerlink Distribution Services, LLC.

All notations of errors or omissions should be addressed to Studio Fun International,
Editorial Department, at the above address.

ISBN: 978-0-7944-4573-7
Manufactured, printed, and assembled in Dongguan, China.
First printing, July 2019. RRD/07/19
23 22 21 20 19   1 2 3 4 5

Disney

MICKEY MOUSE
ADVENTURES

CONTENTS

COWBOY MICKEY

Mickey Mouse was very busy packing his suitcase.

"Hurry!" urged Minnie. "I can't wait to get to the Lucky Star Dude Ranch."

"I'm excited, too!" Mickey told her. "I've always wanted to learn how to ride a horse!"

"And I've always wanted to be a cowgirl!" said Minnie.

Just then Goofy raced in with his suitcase. "I'm all packed and ready to go!" he shouted. "I'm ready to learn how to ride and to twirl a lasso so I can perform in the Lucky Star Rodeo!"

"Is there really going to be a rodeo at the ranch?" asked Minnie.

"That's what I heard," said Mickey. "Wouldn't it be great if we could all be in it?"

"Yes," agreed Minnie. "Let's try!"

"Would you folks like some riding lessons?" said the owner of the ranch as they arrived. "Call me Cowboy Bob, and let me show you the right way to get on a horse."

He held the horses' reins as he helped Mickey, Minnie, and Goofy step up and on to their horses.

"Hey, that wasn't hard at all," bragged Goofy. "Now I'm ready to learn how to use a lasso."

"Lassoing takes a lot of practice," said Cowboy Bob, and he gave Goofy his first lesson.

That night, Mickey and Minnie and some of the ranch hands had a cookout under the stars.

"Yippee-ti-yi-yo!" they all sang around the campfire.
Suddenly they heard a wild cry and saw a strange shadow.
"I think it's a coyote!" whispered Mickey.

Quickly, Cowboy Bob shone his flashlight at the shadow.

"It's not a coyote—it's Goofy!" said Minnie with a giggle. "He's walking on his hands and knees!"

"I fooled you, didn't I?" said Goofy, who was laughing and laughing.

The next day, Mickey and Minnie practiced their riding while Goofy practiced with his lasso.

"You're learning very fast," Cowboy Bob told Mickey and Minnie. "I'll bet you'll be good enough to perform in the rodeo."

"How about me?" asked Goofy. "Whoops!" he cried as he roped his own foot. "I'd better practice some more."

Finally the day of the big rodeo arrived, and Cowboy Bob said they could all perform.

"Let's all line up for the grand rodeo parade!" shouted Cowboy Bob.

"Where's Mickey?" asked Minnie. "I haven't seen him anywhere."

"I don't know," said Goofy. "I haven't seen him either."

At that very moment, Mickey was asleep! He'd forgotten
to set his alarm clock to wake up in time for the rodeo. But
as the crowds passed his window on their way to the rodeo,
their talking woke him up.

When Mickey realized how late he'd slept, he knew he had
to hurry or he'd miss the rodeo.

Mickey got dressed as fast as he could and dashed out the door. "I'd better take all the shortcuts I can," he thought as he raced across a field and jumped over a fence.

"Uh-oh," Mickey groaned. "I think I shouldn't have jumped over that last fence."

Mickey had just landed on a bucking bronco in the middle of the rodeo area!

Everyone cheered as Mickey held tightly to the reins, riding the bronco. "This is sort of fun!" thought Mickey, and then he waved his hat to the crowd.

"Ladies and gentlemen," called the rodeo announcer, "Mickey Mouse just broke the ranch record for the longest time riding a bronco."

The crowd cheered again.

When Mickey jumped off the bronco, it began to chase him. "What do I do now?" shouted Mickey.

"I'll lasso him for you," yelled Goofy, but he lassoed Mickey instead.

However, seeing Mickey all roped up was such a funny sight, even the bucking bronco stopped for a chuckle.

Then Mickey quickly untied himself and raced away.

Everybody cheered as Cowboy Bob presented the rodeo ribbons.

Minnie won for being the best cowgirl and taking good care of the horses.

Mickey won for his bronco riding.

And Goofy won for trying to lasso anything and everything in sight!

25

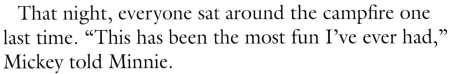

That night, everyone sat around the campfire one
last time. "This has been the most fun I've ever had,"
Mickey told Minnie.

"Me, too," she said with a sigh.

Just then, they all saw an odd profile against the full
moon.

"I'll bet it's just Goofy joking again," said Mickey.

"Nope! I'm sitting right here," said Goofy.

"Then it's a real coyote!" shouted Mickey. "Now I truly feel like a cowboy. Cowboys and coyotes go together."

"Do you want me to lasso him?" asked Goofy.

"No thanks," they all said as they laughed.

MICKEY AND THE FIRE TRUCK

"Let's paint stripes on the old engine!" Huey exclaimed.
Mickey Mouse laughed. "Hold it!" he said, "we still want it to look like a fire truck!"
Mickey and the boys were on their way to the fire station. They had offered to decorate an antique fire truck for the Town Day parade the next day.

"Uncle Donald is working on a top-secret parade float,"
said Louie. "He won't let us see it."

"Don't worry," Mickey answered. "Our fine old truck will
be the pride of the parade."

Mickey and the others arrived just in time to see their friend Goofy slide down the brass pole in the middle of the fire station.

"Hi-ya, gang," said Goofy.

"Goofy is a junior volunteer, just like me," Mickey told the boys, as he leaned over to pat a friendly Dalmatian. "This is Freckles, the fire station's mascot."

"Here's our parade engine." Goofy grinned as he led the boys to an old-fashioned pumper truck. "Isn't she a beauty?" Mickey started polishing the truck while Goofy and the boys went to work on the decorations.

"Does this truck still work?" asked one of the boys.
Mickey nodded. "Yes it works, but it's not as fast or
powerful as the new engines. Now we just use it for parades."

"It must be hard work being a firefighter," Louie said. "It sure is," Goofy responded proudly. "Do you remember when the big hotel caught fire? We had to rescue about twenty people. I even saved Mrs. Porter's parakeet."

"Gosh, Goofy," said Mickey, "If I remember right, the regular firefighters rescued the parakeet. They just gave it to you to hold."

"But I was a big help," Goofy insisted. "I went and found Mrs. Porter and gave her back her bird."

"I'll tell you another story," Goofy said to the boys. "A couple of years ago there was a big fire in the park outside town."

"We had to save the woods from being burnt to the
ground." Goofy said proudly.

"I remember that night," said Mickey. "It was cold and you
and I handed out blankets. I don't remember anything else.

Goofy looked embarrassed and didn't say anything else.
They finished decorating the fire truck and headed home. All
of them were looking forward to the big parade the next day.

The following day, the whole town turned out to watch the parade. The antique truck led the way with Mickey at the wheel. The boys were allowed to ride in the back with Goofy.

"We're going to win the blue ribbon for best parade entry," said Huey. "Uncle Donald's float doesn't have a chance."

FIRE SAFETY

Donald's float was just behind the fire truck. He had mounted a spaceship on his old pick-up truck.

"Hey, Donald!" someone called from the crowd. "Is that a real rocket ship?"

"Almost," Donald answered proudly. "Get a good look. My float is going to send the judges to the moon."

Donald drove his wobbly rocket on down the street, sparks flying everywhere.

Suddenly, the rocket caught fire, and within seconds the whole float was in flames.

"Help!" squawked Donald. "Fire!"

"I'll save you!" Goofy cried. As Mickey pulled to a stop, Goofy grabbed one of the old truck's hoses and hooked it to a nearby hydrant. Then he began spraying Donald's float with water. Before long, the fire was completely out.

Goofy was a hero at last.

During the award ceremony after the parade, the mayor asked him to come forward.

"Goofy, I'd like you to accept this blue ribbon with our thanks." said the mayor, "You were very brave today. In fact, you're the bravest junior volunteer who ever held a hose!"

MICKEY AND THE PET SHOP

"Have a good time!" called Mickey. Mr. Palmer was leaving for an overnight trip and he asked Mickey to take care of his pet shop while he was gone.

"This will be a snap!" Mickey said.

"A snap!" repeated Mr. Palmer's pet parrot.

Mickey gazed at the cuddly pets and colorful fish. They all seemed content—all but one, that is. A cute little puppy was whining and whimpering in the saddest way.

"Poor little fella," said Mickey. "What you need is some attention."

Mickey lifted the puppy from the kennel.
"Steady, boy." said Mickey. But the lively puppy wriggled free and raced over to the goldfish bowl for a drink.

"Watch out!" screeched the parrot.
But he was too late. The bowl tumbled to the floor
with a crash!

"Uh-oh!" cried Mickey.

"Crash! Crash!" squawked the bird, furiously flapping his wings.

"Gotcha!" Mickey caught the fish just in time and put it in a new bowl.

"Try not to cause any more trouble," Mickey said to the lively little puppy.

Just then, he heard the door open and in walked his first customer of the day.

"How can I help you?" Mickey asked.

But before the customer could answer, the puppy darted over to a cage and accidentally opened the door, setting all the mice inside free!

"Eek! I'll come back later. Much later!" cried the customer as she raced for the door.

With the puppy safely back in his cage, Mickey settled down for the evening. But later that night, the puppy howled at the top of his lungs. Mickey covered his ears with a pillow, but it didn't help.

It wasn't long before the puppy got exactly what he wanted—a cozy spot under the covers, right next to Mickey!

When Mickey woke up the next morning, the store was a mess! Mickey knew this must have been the mischevious puppy's doing.

"Oh, well," sighed Mickey, "I guess I'd better start cleaning up before Mr. Palmer gets back."

As Mickey started to work, he noticed the puppy trotting along beside him, helping out wherever he could.

"You may be a rascal," said Mickey, "but I am getting used to having you around."

Mickey and the puppy worked together as a team all day long, tidying the books, cleaning the counters, and dusting the shop floor.

Mickey had just finished cleaning up when in strode Mr. Palmer.

"It looks like everything went smoothly," he said, handing Mickey his pay check.

"Easy as pie," replied a very tired Mickey.

Mickey was just about to leave when the puppy began to howl and scratch at the door of his kennel.

"I'm going to miss you too, little fella," said Mickey sadly.

Suddenly, Mickey thought of the perfect solution. He'd take the puppy instead of his pay!

Everybody was very happy, especially the parrot, who screeched, "And don't come back!"

"But what should I call you?" Mickey wondered when they got outside.

Just then, he saw a newspaper headline: NEW PICTURES OF PLANET PLUTO!

"That's it! I'll call you Pluto!" exclaimed Mickey.

Pluto gave his new master a big wet kiss, and from that day on Mickey and Pluto were the best of friends.

The End